TIME TRAVEL
TRAVEL
Telephone

TIME TRAVEL
Telephone

Lis Jardine

Illustrated by
Alexandra Pulga

Collins

Chapter 1

I'm quite used to being home alone. When I'm off school – which is often, as any kind of bug goes straight to my dodgy lungs and can turn very nasty – I stay in bed taking extra antibiotics, watching TV and sleeping for days. Dad works from home, checking in on me at least once an hour, but it's still lonely without my friends (they're totally banned from visiting me when I'm ill, in case they bring more germs).

Being home alone in the summer holidays, when I'm perfectly well and itching with boredom, is even more annoying than that. All the gang are away – Letty's in France, Gabriela's camping in Devon, and Nilam's family is taking their American cousins on a trip round Scotland – and Dad's knee-deep in one of his Big Projects. My big brother, Nik, is around – but he's spending most of his time in his room listening to loud music while he waits for uni to start.

So, it's just me, and I'm not allowed to go anywhere on my own Just In Case I get an attack of hay fever, or meet a dog (I have allergies), or any other unlikely thing happens to make me get sick. This is because I have cystic fibrosis – or maybe CF has me. It's a condition I was born with that makes my lungs and digestive system sick, and it also makes everyone super protective.

The thing is, I'm not one of those delicate storybook heroines who faints onto their couch every five minutes (OK, I am a tiny bit delicate in body, but definitely not in mind). I get Seriously Bored stuck at home, even with tons of books to read and the internet and TV to look at. I'm supposed to do masses of exercise to clear the gunk in my lungs, but there are only so many times you can jump on the trampoline before you start getting totally fed up.

I want to Do Something, and Dad's too busy working in his office at the end of the garden to take me anywhere fun. As for Nik … he'd never notice I was bored. None of my friends are back for another week, and by then it'll be nearly the start of term at secondary. Which, honestly, I'm not really looking forward to.

It's got to the point where even this house is looking interesting. It used to be a village police station so it's pretty old, with lots of little nooks and crannies. We've only lived here a year, so Dad's still in the middle of decorating, and he often wonders if there are any undiscovered spaces. He reckons the outside is very slightly bigger than the inside … but I don't think he'll ever get around to doing a proper search, not when there are emails to read and spreadsheets to build.

Yesterday, I went round the outside with Dad's big metal tape measure, and today I'm going to do a complete room-by-room exploration of the inside by myself. I'll need to be a bit careful of dust (I should definitely not inhale any) but I'm starting in the front hall and going all the way up to the loft.

I grab a face mask – one of the good ones that filters out the tiniest particles, not those fabric things everyone had in lockdown – and I get to work in the hallway. It's big, and all the downstairs rooms open off it. I already know there's nothing interesting in there – Dad stripped the walls and repainted only a few months ago, so all I do is press the panels at the bottom of the stairs to see if there's a cupboard hidden underneath.

There isn't.

The next room is the kitchen, and I open cabinet after cabinet to push on the backs and sides. Nothing shifts. No surprises.

Then I go to the wall where our big corkboard hangs, covered with notes about school events and hospital appointments. I carefully take it down and look at the big, panelled area of wall behind it. When I explored outside yesterday, this was the bit of the building that seemed a bit different from the shape on the inside.

Steadily, I push at every corner, knot and dent in the wood, standing on a chair to get to the top and working my way down to the bottom. It's getting me nowhere, and I'm starting to think about making myself a snack instead, when there's a funny crunching noise under my fingers.

"Hey up," I whisper to myself. That's what my Yorkshire grandad says when he's surprised.

I push hard again at the same spot and there's a bigger crunch; a tiny crack appears, snaking up the wall several centimetres.

My breath starts to come a little faster. This is it! I press until the crack travels up the wall and along the ceiling. I grab a metal spatula from the drawer and run it along the crumbling paintwork, forcing the thin steel into the growing gap, wedging it in and bending it back and forth until I can get my hands in properly.

Three hard pulls and a large, thin sheet of wood comes away and drops to the floor. Dad's going to be so angry, but I don't care.

I've found something. Something amazing.

Chapter 2

I'm glad I wore the mask; the contents of the hidden space behind the wall are thick with dust. It goes back maybe 30 centimetres – the length of a ruler – and it has two shelves.

First off, on the bottom one there's a telephone. It's squat and square, with a separate, handle-shaped mouthpiece joined to the base with a curly wire. It's dark red and the numbers 1 to 9, then 0, are written on a circle in the middle, with holes over each number to put your finger in and spin the rotary dial.

I've seen ones like it in old films and on "vintage" mood boards online. Never in real life before. I reach out a finger and touch it, leaving a clean dot in

the grime. It's warmish and smooth, and made of plastic. Next to the phone, there's a small spiral-bound notepad, so thickly coated in grey fluff I can't see if anything's written on it.

Above it is the other shelf, lined with old books labelled *Telephone Directory 1976*, with the names of different local areas on them: Swinwood, Macklemere, Fursefield.

On the wall behind, there's just old, peeling

magnolia-coloured paint. Even so, I feel like I've found buried treasure.

What do I do now? Should I go and grab Dad, make him share the discovery whether he likes it or not? Take photos and send them to the group chat? Or … I could take a few minutes to see what exactly I've found all by myself.

I take a few pics but obviously it's way too interesting to wait. I reach out and pick up the notepad, wiping off the dust with one swipe of my hand.

There's a number written on the first page: Mm 36981.

My fingers itch. I've never actually "dialled" a number, but I've seen online videos of people my age trying to figure it out. Before I know it, I've lifted the heavy receiver and put it to my ear. There's a deep, warm buzzing, tempting me. It almost sounds alive.

What harm could it do? That's not even a real phone number these days; there are too few digits.

I put my index finger into the "3" and try to push it round; it only moves with difficulty, and in one direction – clockwise – but I persist and get it right round to the metal stopper.

When I lift my finger out, it whirs back to where it started. This is very satisfying.

Next it's 6; then 9 (which is the furthest round, so takes ages and makes my finger hurt). 8 – 1. There!

A click; an empty silence. Then a voice crackles in my ear, sending a shiver up my spine. A whisper, close by but at the same time impossibly distant.

This is Mrs Portendorfer. There's someone here – an intruder. I can hear them in the kitchen. Could you send an officer, please? I don't have much to steal, but I'm all alone and I can't ... oh dear – [CLUNK]

The voice is cut off, and the buzzing tone returns.

I stare in shock at the telephone handset. I've never heard a voice like that in real life; very posh and clipped. Like one of the old black and white Shakespeare films they made us watch at the end of term – Received Pronunciation, Mrs Routledge called it. Old-fashioned.

That old phone must have been there when our house was a police station – and what I'd just heard sounded a lot like an emergency call.

I go out into the garden and knock on the office door, pushing it open a crack. "Dad?" I call quietly through the gap. He hates it when I walk straight in, in case he's on a video call.

"What do you need, Annie?" he says.

I can tell that he's in the middle of something, but I push my whole head in anyway. "I've found a secret cupboard in the kitchen! And there's an old phone and you have to twizzle all the numbers round and I rang the number, and it was really strange! There was this voice, and she said there was an intruder but then it got cut off! Do you want to see it?"

Dad looks up at me, but his eyes don't really focus. "OK, Annie. Sounds fun, but I'm totally swamped for now. Go and see if Nik will look at your telephone thing. Or write a story about it."

Typical! He didn't even listen properly. Still, he's given me an idea; I go up to my room and search for an old exercise book I hardly started in Year Five. It's got tons of spare lined pages, so I take it downstairs, borrow the kitchen pen and try to write down exactly what Mrs Portendorfer said. It feels important.

Chapter 3

Mysteries are my favourite type of book to read. I've got loads, and I swap them with Gabriela and Nilam all the time: *A Terribly Modest Murder*, *Death on the Tracks*, *Ellie Investigates* … I can't get enough. And if this isn't a case – a mystery to solve – then I don't know what is.

When you're detecting, you must do research, of course. You can't just sit there; you have to go looking for clues. The first thing I think of is to look in the old telephone directories on the shelf in the secret alcove, because the internet isn't going to know who'd had that old phone number.

The letters Mm had been written in front of the telephone number, so I carefully lift down the Macklemere book. Macklemere is my village and "Mm" must stand for that. The directory is really bashed, so when this house was a police station, they must have used this one the most. It's all creased and rumpled, but I quickly turn to the P's and run my finger down the page.

Podmore, J
Pollard, Y
Polson, L
Poole, S
Popham, H
Portendorfer, M . . . 3 Willow Av, Mmere

Willow Avenue is so close! Only maybe three streets away, and on the way to the shop …

"Annie? What did you do?"

I haven't heard Nik coming, and here he is, staring accusingly at the mess I've made.

"Oh hi, Nik," I say, trying to sound chill. "Just found this really cool phone. From when the house was a police station."

Nik comes over and inspects the dusty cupboard.

"I'm not sure I'd call it cool. You're in SO MUCH TROUBLE when Dad sees this."

"No, but listen," I say. "There's a message on it."

Nik raises his eyebrows. "A message? That's not an answerphone."

I sigh. "No – it plays when you dial the number on the notepad. Look, hold the handset up to your ear and I'll do it. It's totally a call from the past."

Nik shrugs. "Go on then. I'll believe it when I hear it." He picks up the handset, and I repeat my turns of the dial.

Nik's face loses its smug know-it-all look as Mrs Portendorfer's voice begins to speak. His eyes widen when the call is cut off. "How did you do that?" he says. He checks around the phone. "Have you wired it up to your smartphone or – "

"No! It's for real. From the past. And I've looked up Mrs Portendorfer in the old phone book, see, and she lived at number 3 Willow Avenue. We could go and have a look, if you're not busy?"

Nik grunts. "You've got to be kidding. This is a trick."

I look him straight in the eye. "No, it isn't. I promise. What if she still lives there and remembers making the call?"

Nik looks back at the telephone in the dusty cupboard. "Hmm." He seems to shake himself a little. "We *could* go to the corner shop and swing past Willow Avenue on the way."

This is the first time Nik's volunteered to take me anywhere this summer, and I'm not going to waste it. I dash upstairs, grab my bag, and shoot out of the front door in record time. Unfortunately, then I have to wait five minutes while Nik puts on his shoes and writes a note for Dad, which he leaves on the kitchen table.

The corner shop isn't far. We reach the end of our street and pass two more on the way to Willow Avenue; it's one of the longest roads in Macklemere, all detached Victorian houses, with big gardens and wide drives. There are tall trees all along the pavement, bright with green leaves which rustle in the breeze.

"Right," Nik says, "you go and look at your very interesting road. I'll meet you back here in five minutes."

Number 3 is probably the smartest house I can see. Newly painted wooden windows, a deep blue front door, and beds full of colourful flowers. I stand just outside the gate; I'm not quite sure I've got the nerve to walk up and ring that shiny brass doorbell.

"What are you doing?" comes a voice I am absolutely not expecting.

Chapter 4

Standing at the end of the drive at number 1 is Mrs Finch, who I know well; she works in the office at my old primary school.

"Are you looking for Mr Gray, Annie? I probably wouldn't bother, if you're fundraising for Scouts or something like that. He's ever so grouchy and he doesn't like kids much."

I blink twice. "Mr Gray? I thought – "

"Very fussy man! He's a book dealer – he sells old and expensive books. Hates nosy parkers, too, so I shouldn't stand staring at his house for long!" Mrs Finch turns to go back along her drive.

I think hard about whether to take this

investigation any further. I was hoping to find Mrs Portendorfer and ask her what had happened … a grumpy old man wouldn't be great fun to disturb. But I don't have time to think for too long – Nik will be on his way back any minute.

I step quickly onto the drive and walk up to the front door and press the bell.

I wait, nibbling a nail. Then the door is swung wide open and there, I guess, is Mr Gray, standing in front of a dark hallway lined with bookshelves. He looks down his long nose at me and folds his arms. "Yes? What do you want?"

I gulp. Mrs Finch was right. I put on my most polite expression and ask the only question I can think of (with a tiny bit of pretending to disguise my reasons for asking).

"Hello, I'm doing some research into the neighbourhood for school, and I wondered if you could tell me anything about Mrs Portendorfer, who used to live here."

Mr Gray's left eyelid twitches. "Never heard of her. And I've lived here for 48 years. So, mind your own business and be off!"

He turns away back into the house and slams the door behind him. I stand staring at the door for a few seconds, confused. Surely the directory can't have been wrong. It had looked very official, and it was published by the telephone company.

Mrs Finch is still in her front garden, picking dead heads off the roses. "That sounded like a bit of a growl. What did you ask him?"

"I was looking for someone who used to live here. Do *you* remember Mrs Portendorfer?"

"Oh yes," Mrs Finch replies. "From when I was little. Margery was lovely, quite a bit older than I am now, and a widow. She always let me play with her doll collection when I brought her post round or anything. The dolls were Victorian, and very fragile, but she was so kind. Little Linda, she used to call me."

"That's great! I'm not here for the Scouts – I'm just doing some research on our neighbourhood. I came across the name; it's so unusual – I wondered what anyone knows about her. Do you remember if she ever got burgled, for example?" I smile winningly at Mrs Finch, hoping that it isn't too strange a question.

"Not that I ever heard. It's a quiet, safe street, Willow Avenue. To be honest, she must have moved away suddenly because one day I saw that Mr Gray was living there." Mrs Finch stood up from the rose bush and stretched her back. "I was only small, so I don't remember much, but no one saw a van or anything. I did hear my mother say that Mrs Portendorfer had family in Australia, so perhaps she emigrated? Anyway, Mr Gray will be gone soon. I saw the house listed in the Estate Agent's window, so I guess he's retiring from the book trade. Moving I don't know where, and he's not likely to tell me, either!"

"Thank you, Mrs Finch … I'd better go. I'm meeting my brother on his way back from the shop."

"Just call me Linda! You're not in juniors any more, are you?"

"No," I say, with a little frown. I don't say it, but I'm going to miss primary school, where everyone knows all about me and about CF, and no one stares when I take my pills at lunch time or eat a whole giant protein bar at break. I'm dreading all the strange looks and questions I'm going to get when I start at Swinwood High.

I walk quickly towards the corner and see Nik coming towards me.

"Did you find her then?" he says.

"No, but Mrs Finch from Macklemere Primary

lives next door, and she just told me all kinds of suspicious stuff. Mrs Portendorfer basically disappeared, ages ago."

"You mean she moved out," Nik laughs. "Oh well. Come on, let's go home."

I carry on talking as we walk together. "Actually, she's given me a different thread to follow – Australia. Although I'm not sure where to start."

"Australia? Give over, Annie. She's just an old lady who moved away."

"Explain the phone call from the past, then!"

Nik has nothing to say to that question.

When we get in, there's a note replacing Nik's on the kitchen table.

Kids, I want to know why this wall is in pieces. I'm tied up with online meetings all afternoon, but I'm expecting a complete explanation later! NOT HAPPY.

Dad

Chapter 5

"Told you," Nik says. "Good luck getting away with *that*!" Then he runs upstairs, leaving me alone to face the consequences of making a large hole in the wall. I screw up the note and bin it, as if that's going to help. Then I grab my notebook and write up what I've found out so far.

Mrs Portendorfer
- A neighbour (Mrs Finch) remembers her living there a long time ago, so the phone book was right.
- Mrs Portendorfer lived on Willow Avenue until she was a bit older than Mrs Finch is now (maybe 65+?).
- Mrs Portendorfer's first name is Margery and she was a widow.
- She was nice to Mrs Finch when Mrs F was a child and let her play with her Victorian dolls.

- She left quite suddenly, and no one saw her go.
- Mrs Portendorfer has relatives in Australia.

Mr Gray
- He doesn't know who Mrs Portendorfer is.
- He's lived in the house for 48 years.
- Mrs F says he was the next owner after Mrs Portendorfer and now he's selling the house.
- He works as a book dealer selling expensive books. (There are lots of bookshelves with books in his hallway.)
- He is grumpy, rude, and doesn't like nosy parkers or kids.

The intruder
- No information yet!

I read through the list. It doesn't add up to much. I lean back in the chair feeling deflated. But I don't have to try and solve this all by myself. I pull my smartphone out of my back pocket and send the pictures I took of the old telephone and my notes, to Letty, Gabriela and Nilam on our group chat.

Hey, everyone! Hope you're enjoying your holidays. I've got a little mystery going here … Any ideas?

Of course, I have to explain the whole situation.

My thumbs hurt by the time I'm done messaging.

Letty refuses to believe that I heard a voice from the past: she's always been very rational and scientific.

I think you're winding us up. Cool vintage phone though.

Gabriela (who reads ghost stories and thrillers) reckons I'm in danger.

Don't go anywhere in the dark! Or open any locked rooms. I think Mr Gray is definitely a baddie and you need to be mega careful so you don't end up hurt xxx

Nilam is more helpful, as I would expect from a fellow detective fan (who also believes in the paranormal).

If you want to know more about local history and the people who've lived here in the past, there are lots of websites. The local History Society in Macklemere probably has one. Or you could look at the family tree research sites, or the registry of births and deaths? Maybe the police have records of burglaries.

I go into the living room and grab my tablet. That's what I use to chat to other CF kids online. People with CF are strictly forbidden to meet each other in real life, because of the risk of catching each other's bugs (we grow particularly bad ones in our lungs), so it's the only way to talk to people who REALLY know what living with CF is like. I'm one of the unlucky ones – I don't have the right kind of cystic fibrosis for *modulators*, which are amazing modern drugs that can really, really help with CF – so swapping stories with other kids like me is super important.

Time to try out Nilam's suggestions. "Births and Deaths UK" brings up an archive website and lets me type in the name Margery Portendorfer. I quite quickly find a record of Mrs Portendorfer's marriage (26th July 1926, Wombourne) to a man named Michael. The certificate lists her unmarried name as Margery Melville – and it's a hyperlink!

I click through and the site shows me a page listing other documents related to Margery Melville/Portendorfer – as well as the marriage certificate, there's her birth certificate (13th January 1905, Staffordshire). But nothing else.

I take a screenshot of the list page and send it directly to Nilam.

Hmm. What's on Mr Portendorfer's page? Nilam texts back.

I check it out. There's a birth certificate, the marriage certificate and a death certificate, too – 19th December 1968.

I text Nilam. *There's no record of Mrs Portendorfer's death. According to the official records, she's still alive somewhere … aged 120.*

Nilam replies in seconds.

That doesn't seem likely. Time to test my other idea. Are you feeling brave?

I swallow. Yeah, I am. I search for Macklemere Police, and up pops the local Neighbourhood Team web page. The very first button at the top of the page says, "How can I get in touch?".

I click straight on it and discover a phone number, an email address and an option to start a live web chat. I think about talking to Dad or Nik before I go on, but who could provide better and more trustworthy information than the police?

So, I start a chat. I have to put in my name and work my way through a few I-am-not-a-robot questions before I actually get to ask the question that's burning at the tip of my fingers.

"Do you have details of missing people from the 70s?"

I wait for a response, one, two minutes. Finally, three dots appear in the chat, showing that someone is typing at the other end.

"I'm sorry, we don't keep records that long in our live system. You might find archived information by contacting the UK Missing Persons Unit."

They give me a phone number which I don't bother to copy down. I'm definitely not ready to *ring up* an official government department. I don't think Nik will do it for me either. Now that I think about it, Mrs Finch would have mentioned it if there'd been any official fuss about Mrs Portendorfer disappearing at the time.

So that's a dead end.

Chapter 6

I hear the back door open. Dad's probably come in for coffee.

"Annie Edwards! Explain this mess!" He's looking at the splintered edges of the gap. "Why on earth did you pull this board off without asking me first? Now I'm going to have to redecorate in here, after I've fixed the damage to the wall."

"Don't you care about that cool old telephone and the shelves? They've been hidden here for yonks and yonks, maybe since before you were even born. How's that not interesting?"

Dad lets out a sigh. "I don't find dusty, ancient rubbish particularly interesting, especially when the discovery means more DIY work that I don't have time to do. The best thing I can say about this is that the vintage phone might make a few pounds on an auction website."

"Well, I *am* sorry." I can't hold my irritation in. "I think it's totally amazing. That phone played me a message FROM THE PAST! Like … like magic, or time travel or something! And now I'm looking for the lady who made that call, back – I think – 50ish years ago, because she was in trouble, and it doesn't sound like anyone's seen her since, so it's the most important thing I've done all summer!"

At this point, Nik comes down to enjoy the commotion, standing grinning in the doorway and making faces at me. It makes me even crosser.

"And you just sit in your office sending boring emails to boring work people, and leaving me to try and entertain myself for six BORING weeks!"

"You're talking absolute nonsense, Annie, and I just don't have time for it. Go back to the living room and watch something sensible – like a nature documentary – on TV."

"It's not nonsense! It really happened, and there's a real mystery! What do I have to do ... to ... convince ... you?"

By the end of the last sentence, my voice has become thick and croaky. I try to keep them down, but my body's soon wracked with coughs, nasty phlegmy ones, the sticky kind that only people with CF get.

"Hey, hey," Dad jumps up to pass me his glass of water. "That's what comes of getting over-excited. Here, sip. And let's do some physio."

Physio is one of the most boring things I have to do with my CF, but sitting with Dad as I work through some breathing exercises (which I could do by myself, but he likes to "help"... a legacy from when I was little and he needed to do physio for me), does actually help me bring up the sticky mucus that my lungs make.

Nik's lost his grin, but he knows the routine. He helps guide me back into the living room, gets me some water and tissues and sits quietly while I begin to breathe deeply to get air behind my mucus and push it out of my lungs.

"There, that's better."

Before long I've coughed up a chunk of gunk and spit it out into a tissue. "Thanks," I say.

"You look awful. Can I suggest you go to bed for an hour?"

"I'm 11 years old, Dad! I don't need a nap – "

Nik backs Dad up, typically. "Annie. You've been a bit unpredictable today. You need to take a deep breath and sort yourself out."

"Humour us," Dad says, looking sternly into my watering eyes. "Read a book or something if you like, but just – have a rest. That was a tiring coughing fit."

"OK," I shrug. "But I'm not kidding about the investigation. Are either of you going to listen properly and HELP me?"

Dad runs a hand through his curls. "We can talk about it later. I've still got four hours' work to do today. You get under your duvet for a bit."

Nik shrugs, avoiding looking directly at me. He knows that call wasn't made up – he heard the voice from the past himself, so he can't just pretend everything's normal.

I stomp upstairs and lie down. When I wake, it's 5 o'clock and the sun's shining in through the windows. I stretch and roll out of bed, feeling considerably better after the rest (although I won't tell Dad he was right, obviously).

I go downstairs and find Dad sitting at the kitchen table, mug in hand, staring at the old phone in the wall. "You done working yet?" I ask.

"Yes. So now you need to tell me the whole story, please, right from the beginning!"

Chapter 7

"I don't know," Dad says, after I've filled him in and showed him my notebook. "That's not really a believable story, Annie. That old phone shouldn't even be connected to a landline any more – it's been walled off in a cupboard for so long – "

"I heard it too, Dad," says Nik, coming into the kitchen. "And no. It shouldn't still be wired up to the network. Maybe it's not technology, though. Maybe it's something … something less explainable."

Nik's obviously been listening to the conversation. He hasn't paid me this much attention all summer.

Dad sighs. "I'm not interested in getting

caught up in something that's imaginary. And even if it's true, it's totally not our business."

"It is our business! Aren't we supposed to look out for other people – help them when they're in distress? It doesn't look like anyone paid attention to Mrs Portendorfer's original call, did they?" I'm piling on the pressure; now Nik is backing me up, it's two against one and Dad's got no chance. "Why don't you try ringing the number? It already worked for me and Nik. See if you can repeat the outcome – that's how a scientist checks their trial results, isn't it?"

Dad looks at me, then at the old red phone again, for a long moment. "OK. That seems like a fair test."

We all go over to the cavity in the wall, and I pick up the handset. "You hold this, and I'll dial."

"Let me," Nik says. I raise an eyebrow.

"I've never used one before," he says, defensively.

"Oh!" Dad hears the low buzz from the earpiece. "It *has* got a connection."

"Told you," I say. Nik slowly moves the heavy dial mechanism over and over again. We wait for a few seconds before Dad's eyes suddenly open to their fullest. Mrs Portendorfer's voice, tinny and quiet, is the only sound in the kitchen as she makes her plea for help.

... I'm all alone and I can't ... oh dear – [CLUNK]

Dad holds the phone handset away from his face and stares into it. "The connection's gone," he whispers. "Listen – no tone."

"Maybe it only plays once for each listener?" I say. It's a total guess, but Nik nods in agreement.

Dad shrugs and puts down the receiver. "Maybe. But … that definitely happened." He looks at me, frowning slightly.

"Don't you need to say, 'Sorry, Annie, I was wrong to doubt you. I'll make you pizza for tea?'" I'm joking. Although pizza would be nice.

"OK, why don't you two go and see if there's anything in this Australian connection. Maybe Mrs Portendorfer went there. The internet's a global network of people, and you might come across a relative – Portendorfer is an unusual name."

I get the tablet and type "Portendorfer Australia" into the search bar. There are a few family-tree type results, but my eye is drawn to the first entry in the list. A profile on Friendbox, for Toni Portendorfer, Fitness Centre Manager.

I'm definitely not allowed to have my own social media accounts, but Dad's logged in already, so I can click through and take a look at the little information she makes public. Toni Portendorfer works at a public gym in Queensland, and lists her interests as crocheting, local history and DIY.

"That could be a relative," I say.

Nik leans in and taps a menu button in the top corner of the screen. "Come on, let's message her. See if she's related."

"Hadn't we better check with Dad first? It's his Friendbox account."

Nik rolls his eyes but jumps up and goes into the kitchen. He's back almost immediately. "Dad says go for it. We're not going to offend anyone by asking."

"What do I say? She's not going to believe all the time travelling phone call business, is she?" I say.

"Make it simple. Just, 'Hi, we're doing local history research and came across your unusual surname here in Macklemere – do you know anything about Margery who lived here in the 1970s?' That should do the trick."

I type almost that exact sentence into the

direct message box, then click the button. "Sent. Wonder what the time is in Oz?"

Nik takes the tablet, opens up a new search tab and looks it up. "Queensland. Ah. It's 2 o'clock in the morning there. I guess we might hear something tomorrow, then."

"Let's tell Dad." We head into the kitchen and bring Dad up to date.

"OK. Now, set the table for pizza. I found one in the freezer, but we'll have a big salad with it."

"Ace," I say, and Nik and I start raiding the drawer for cutlery.

"I still can't believe you've trashed that wall," Dad mutters, as he opens the fridge door.

That evening we watch an old film together with our plates of pizza and have chocolate biscuits dunked in tea for dessert. I text Nilam with the new info and send him a screenshot of Toni's Friendbox page.

Great detecting, Annie! Just wish I was there to help.

I wish he was here too. And that Letty was less of a sceptic. Although, it's kind of fun having Nik help me with the case.

I go to bed at half past 9 in the evening, knowing it's the quickest way to get to the morning and a possible reply from Toni Portendorfer. I do my nebuliser (another twice a day thing) which delivers medications straight into my lungs and repeat my breathing exercises to make sure I'm gunge-free and have a decent night.

I set my alarm for 7 o'clock and settle down on my heaped-up pillows to read *Izzie Irvine Investigates!*

Chapter 8

Nik beats me to the tablet next morning. It's Saturday, so he doesn't usually get up early, but I guess he's finally caught the bug of this investigation as much as I have.

"Message!" he yells up the stairs to me, while I'm still in the bathroom.

I wash my hands at top speed and crash down the stairs two at a time to see what Toni has said.

"Hello," it reads. "Portendorfer is an unusual name, yes! I did have a Great Auntie Margery, as it happens, who lived in the British Midlands, but I never knew her. Maybe we could talk? We have the technology! I'll send you a link."

Below this is a long and complicated link that will take us to an online meeting service, the kind that Dad uses at work all the time.

"That's so cool! I wonder what she knows," I say. Dad joins us and I tap the link. The blank screen is replaced by a middle-aged, tanned woman with lots of friendly smile lines around her eyes and mouth.

"Hi! You just caught me. What's all this about Great Auntie Marge, eh? Haven't heard her name in ages. She can't still be alive, can she? She was an old woman when I was a kid."

"Um, I found her date of birth," I say. "She'd be about 120 now, so I guess not. But I'm doing a research project for school, and I just wondered if you knew what had happened to her?"

"WE wondered," Dad corrected. "There doesn't seem to be any record of her in the UK since the mid-70s. Did she emigrate to Australia after that, or – "

Toni's shaking her head. "She didn't come here,

that's for sure," she says. "I was hoping you might have some info about her yourselves, to be honest. Mum had a bit of a falling-out with her about some paintings that belonged to Uncle Michael's family. We stopped hearing from Auntie Marge, must have been around that sort of date, and letters to her place didn't get any answers. We never heard that there was a funeral or anything, but Mum just assumed she'd died, I think, although Mum did say *she* ought to have inherited some of Uncle Michael's books."

"Books?" I ask, my heart beating a little faster.

"Auntie Marge's husband was a big collector, rare books and the like, and of course she would have kept hold of them while she lived in that amazing old house of hers." Toni shrugged. "I've got photos, somewhere. Some of his stuff was worth thousands, I reckon, let alone the house."

I can just smell a motive for a burglary now, and I'm desperate to discuss it with Nik and Dad.

"Well," Dad says. "We've really only just started our research. If we find anything definite out, we'll be in touch. Do you have any documents or names, dates we might find useful?"

"I'll see if Mum had any papers; I've got some of her old boxes in the attic. And I can scan those pictures of Aunt Margery's house for you now and send them over."

"Brilliant. Well, goodnight, Toni!"

"Yeah, and good morning to you! Have a nice brekkie!" Toni waves and disconnects the call.

"Awesome," I say. "I saw a lot of books in the front hall when I spoke to Mr Gray … do you think it's a coincidence? I mean, Mrs Finch said he was some kind of book dealer – antiques?"

"Did she? Well, I guess that might mean something. But it doesn't really feel like it gets us anywhere. Where did Mrs Portendorfer go?" Dad's expression is worried. "Look, I've got some work to get on with. I'll have a think about what we should do next – "

Nik and I share a look. It's clear neither of us are in the mood to wait around.

Chapter 9

Once Dad has gone, Nik taps at the tablet nervously. "Something awful could have happened to Mrs Portendorfer ... we should report it. Let the police do their job."

I am feeling a bit queasy about this whole investigation, now that I know for certain that Mrs Portendorfer didn't go to her family in Australia.

"How will we get to the police station?" I ask.

"Walk! It's good exercise. I never made it to the gym yesterday, and you're bored with the trampoline, I can tell."

We both get dressed, and I take my tablets and eat a high calorie breakfast of peanut butter and jam on toast to fuel me for the walk. Then Nik and I head off to Swinwood police hub.

We don't say much on the journey. I'm thinking about Mr Gray and how he came to own Mrs Portendorfer's house. Nik is chewing his lip the whole way, and when we arrive at our destination, he clears his throat.

"I'd better do the talking, Annie. I'm not sure the police are great at listening to little kids' theories. So, we'll stick to the facts as we've uncovered them and see what they say. OK?"

I'm not impressed at being described as a little kid. "Sure. But don't be surprised if I correct you when you remember something wrong."

Nik gives a half smile. "I'll do my best to be accurate. Come on."

The police hub is a brand-new building with shiny paintwork and carpets that smell of chemicals. I hope I'm not allergic. There's a reception desk right inside the front door, with a uniformed officer on duty.

"How can we help you today, sir?" The officer barely looks up from the computer screen.

"We want to report something suspicious," Nik says. "Not a recent thing – it happened a while ago."

"Can you narrow it down for me, sir? I need to direct you to the correct department. Is it a missing person, a homicide, robbery – ?"

Nik waves his hands around, trying to come up with the right category. "I mean – possibly a missing person? But it seems to have been a robbery too. Or – "

"Grand larceny?" I suggest. That's a term I've seen on American detective shows which means Stealing Really Expensive Stuff.

The police officer stifles a smirk. "Right you are. If you'll just take a seat in our waiting area, someone will be out to see you shortly."

Nik and I sit together at one end of the row of plastic chairs. There is no one else around, so I don't feel like breaking the silence. The minutes stretch on and I wish I'd brought my book.

Boom! A door swings open on the left and bounces off the wall.

"Grand larceny?" says a woman, with short dark hair and a plain grey suit.

"That'll be us," Nik says.

"Come this way, sir. I'm DI Bell, duty officer for the next … hour or so. Been up all night! Right, here we are, interview room 1. Take a seat and tell me all about it."

Nik and I exchange glances. She seems friendly, but that doesn't mean she's going to listen.

We start to tell DI Bell what we've learnt about Mrs Portendorfer and the situation at 3 Willow Avenue. Neither of us mention the time travelling telephone bit, of course. We're not stupid.

DI Bell writes everything down in a notebook. "So – this woman Margery Portendorfer was living at the Willow Avenue address until the mid-70s, according to an entry in a 1970s phone book and the testimony of the neighbour, but was not seen to leave, and the house has been occupied by a different party, Mr Gray, ever since? And her family hasn't heard from her?"

"And there's no death certificate," I pipe up. "Not online anyway."

"Hmm," DI Bell scratches her ear. "It's interesting, but it doesn't really add up to much, I'm afraid. If she wasn't reported missing and there was no fuss at the time, the chances are that there's a simple explanation. Such as her moving to a different town and selling her house privately."

I bite my lip. I know I can't say anything about the phone call, but the major bit of info DI Bell is missing is Mrs Portendorfer's call for help – her report of the break-in.

Without that, Nik and I have run out of things to say, and DI Bell closes her notebook. "I do appreciate your taking the time to come in and tell me about this, but with no suggestion of foul play and no witnesses, I'm afraid it's not even a cold case. It's a non-case."

DI Bell's smile is pleasant, and she means well, but my heart's sunk to the bottom of my ribcage.

Nik's shoulders slump and he leans back in the chair. "Right. Well, thanks for your time anyway."

DI Bell shakes our hands and sees us out of the hub. We stand on the pavement outside for a couple of minutes, feeling frustrated.

Chapter 10

"That wasn't very useful, was it," I say.

"Nope. I do kind of see her point, though. Let's go home."

Nik decides to take the long way home, for the sake of a few extra steps on his pedometer. The walk takes us down Macklemere High Street, and we're just turning up Victoria Street when I glance in the window of King & Son estate agency and stop.

"What's up?" Nik says.

"She said it's on the market. Mrs Finch, I mean, she said number 3 is for sale. Help me look – it might be listed here."

Nik looks in one window and I look in the other. There are photos of lots of different types of houses: bungalows, semi-detached, and in the bottom left-hand corner, a well-kept Victorian villa that I instantly recognise.

"It's this one! Look," I yelp, and Nik joins me to examine the advert. The price underneath the picture makes us both blink in surprise.

"We should get the brochure," Nik says.

I smile, liking how Nik is getting so invested in our search. "Good idea."

Nik pushes open the estate agency door, which buzzes gently. A man in a suit looks up from his computer, as we shuffle in, and smiles a professional smile. "How can I help you?" he asks.

"Hi. My sister's doing a school project – about houses in the area – " Nik starts, but I'm not letting him do my talking for me here, too.

"Yes, and I'm particularly interested in the period property you have listed – 3 Willow Avenue," I butt in. "Could we possibly have the full details? It'll be great for my presentation."

The man seems to buy the school project idea and reaches into a filing cabinet and extracts a thick wodge of shiny paper. "I'm expecting this one to sell quickly, to be honest – houses on Willow

Avenue don't come up for sale often, and this one's been handsomely restored to its 19th-century glory."

"Thank you," we both murmur, and escape with another little buzz as the door closes behind us.

"Remind me never to become an estate agent," Nik laughs. "He's obviously been doing it so long he speaks like that automatically!"

We look though the photos and descriptions of the rooms as we walk the rest of the way home.

"Looks very posh," I say. The photos show oak panelling, floor-length curtains and four-poster beds.

When we get home, Dad's still in the garden office, so we make ourselves quick cheesy pasta for lunch. I leave Nik loading the dishwasher (his turn) and go into the living room. I swipe idly at the tablet, wondering if Nilam has sent any holiday photos, but instead there's a notification about a new message from Toni Portendorfer on Friendbox.

I shout to the kitchen. "Hey, Nik! Message!" and open up the Friendbox app.

"What is it?" Nik puts his head round the door,

still holding a dirty plate.

"The pics from Toni have come through – look," I say. They show a beautiful house with bookcases on every wall, as well as what look like real oil paintings and tall, Chinese-style vases on the windowsills.

We carefully examine Toni's black and white photos on the screen, which are all slightly fuzzy, and compare them to the estate agency's brochure.

It's very obvious that, although some things have been moved around (I mean – it's been 48 years), some things are the same. The bookcases look identical, and they're filled with the same kind of hardback books. The paintings on the walls are definitely the same ones.

Nik and I exchange a look. "Why are some of Mrs Portendorfer's belongings still in the house?" he says.

Chapter 11

"We should bring Dad up to speed," I say. "Don't you think Mr Gray's involved in Mrs Portendorfer's disappearance?"

"Maybe. Do we have to tell him about us going to the police, though?" Nik says. "He might not be happy about us taking matters into our own hands like that."

"Obviously," I say. "Dad will want to avoid getting sucked in to this if he can. But he'd like to see these pictures, I think."

We head out to the garden office and show Dad all the pictures. But Dad isn't as convinced as us that this means Mr Gray's done anything wrong.

"If she was moving far away or something – she might have included a lot of the contents in the house sale. Which would explain why no one saw a van at the time," Dad says. "I'm not sure that gives us any more to be going on with."

Dad's unwillingness to get involved doesn't surprise me much. I need real proof, something Mrs Portendorfer would never leave behind … maybe, somewhere, those old dolls Mrs Finch talked about are still in the house?

It seems that Nik's thinking very similar thoughts to me. "Shall we go for another walk?" he says. "Slide by Willow Avenue again? I didn't really get much of a look last time."

I give Nik a fist bump. "I am so up for that. But I hope that Mr Gray doesn't see us. He was really rude when I just asked him a simple question!"

Nik grins. "Maybe you ought to put a hat on, then. He might recognise you, but I can just pretend to be looking for number 5."

When we get to Willow Avenue, however,

there are two small surprises. First, number 3's curtains are closed, and the gate is firmly shut. Second, Mrs Finch is out weeding her front garden again and spots us as we cross the road. She gives us a wave.

"Hello, love! Back again? And Nik! Haven't seen you for years, have you finished school now?"

Nik nods but doesn't get a word in before Mrs Finch carries on. "What on earth do you still want with our delightful Mr Gray? He gave you a flea in your ear yesterday – and you've missed him, anyway."

I answer before Nik can open his mouth. "Oh, really? Has he gone out today?"

"There's a big antiquarian book conference in Birmingham this weekend – he goes every year, and he probably won't be back till tomorrow night. You made me think, you know, Annie, after your visit yesterday. I had a good search through my big cupboard and found a photo. Stay there a minute and I'll show you."

Mrs Finch disappears into her house, but

Nik and I don't have time to speak, as she comes hurrying back up her drive straight away.

"I know it's a bit creased, but there's Mrs Portendorfer holding three of her dolls. My mother must have taken it."

I take the small, black and white picture. Mrs Portendorfer has a kind face, and the dolls are very prim and well-dressed. "Wow, thanks, Mrs Finch," I say.

Nik clears his throat. "Is there any chance we could borrow this? It'd be great for Annie's presentation at school – she could scan it and blow it up for the slide show."

"Oh, of course! Although I'll want it back for my album. It's nice to think someone's remembering Mrs P; she was such an old dear. Mind you – she was getting a tiny bit forgetful, sometimes. She used to leave a spare key under one of the flowerpots in the back garden so she could let herself in every time she locked herself out! Anyway, I must get back to the garden."

"Of course! Lovely to talk to you," I say.

Mrs Finch goes back to her flower bed, and we start to walk the short distance home.

As soon as we get out of earshot, Nik blurts out what he's thinking. "Annie, this might be our chance – our only chance – to take a look around and try to find some evidence."

"Nik? Are you OK?" I reach up to his forehead, to see if he's got a fever. "Are you genuinely suggesting we break into that house?"

"Maybe. What if there's still a key there, under a flowerpot or on top of the door frame? We wouldn't do any damage, would we? Just poke around a bit.

Otherwise, that's it. We've done all we can do."

"What if he comes back early? What if there's an alarm? What if – ?" I'm thinking of all the things that could go wrong.

"It's risky. But I didn't see an alarm – I think he's rather too keen on period accuracy, if those sash windows and original doorbell are anything to go by. And Mrs Finch said he won't be back till later tomorrow at the earliest – "

I think for a moment. If we don't do it, Mrs Portendorfer's disappearance might never be solved. And Mr Gray will get away with whatever he's done to her, move away and enjoy all the money he makes from selling her house.

"I'm in," I tell Nik. "No one missed her enough to do anything about it at the time, but she deserves to be found, doesn't she?"

"I think so," he says. "Right. This is going to be a dead of night operation, Annie, so get your darkest clothes ready and maybe have another afternoon nap today!"

Chapter 12

The afternoon is spent in my bedroom, finding the right outfit for a night-time operation. I update my investigation notebook, too, with all the latest discoveries Nik and I have made.

Mrs Portendorfer's house
- The estate agency photographs show lots of old books.
- Toni's photos of the house show lots of old books in the same bookcases.
- Are the books in the two photographs the same?
- If these are Michael Portendorfer's valuable books, why did Mrs Portendorfer leave them?
- Dad says people leave things when they move. Mrs Portendorfer wouldn't leave her dolls, but they're not in the photos.
- Mrs Finch has given us a photograph of the dolls.
- Mr Gray is away for the weekend.

After I've made my notes on the case, I go back onto the tablet and open the group chat; surely Letty and Gabriela will want to be included now I'm so close to confirming there's a real mystery here?

Look – loads of new info that NEARLY PROVES I was right, and Mrs Portendorfer is missing and possibly had all her stuff stolen.

I attach one or two of Toni's photos along with ones from the estate agency, as well as a scan of the dolls photo Mrs Finch gave us. I feel like I'm waiting for ages before Letty replies.

I still don't think you heard a time travelling telephone call, but there are a lot of similarities in the photos, I guess. I can't believe you had the nerve to go to the police on your own!

Maybe I should have mentioned that Nik is helping.

Nilam is next to comment.

What are you going to do next? Not seriously try to break into the house?

It's the only option if we want to find something to get the police interested, I reply. *Nik's coming, obv.*

Gabriela's the last one to reply.

Make sure you have a good plan. And wear gloves! I'd NEVER have the nerve to go out and poke around a strange house at night. Those dolls look really spooky!

That evening, Nik and I discuss our strategy.

"When we're walking to Willow Avenue, we'll need to avoid the streetlights as best we can," Nik said. "If you hear a car coming, stand still in the shadows until it passes."

"Agreed," I said. "And we'll need to tiptoe past number 17, where that noisy poodle lives."

Nik nods, but then looks at me, brow slightly creased. "Don't consider this a criticism in any way, but you'll need to be a bit careful of your lungs. A badly timed coughing fit could be difficult to hide."

"I'll wear my mask. That'll keep the air I'm inhaling a bit warmer and moister."

"Oh!" Nik jumps up from his seat at the kitchen table. "That reminds me – gloves!"

I join him as he searches the bathroom cupboard. There's an old box of disposable gloves from the last time I was very sick, so we each pocket a pair.

I go to bed early and, to my surprise, I get a solid four hours' sleep before my alarm starts blipping. I'm already in my dark clothes instead of my pyjamas, so I'm ready to go in minutes. I debate what to take; in the end, I pocket the picture of Mrs Portendorfer's dolls, and make sure Toni's photos are downloaded from the group chat so I can check them against the actual house. I leave my notebook on the desk in my bedroom.

Nik takes a bit longer, possibly dreading the trip a little more than I am, as well as worrying about waking Dad up.

It's 3 o'clock in the morning when the two of us sneak out of our house. It feels weird getting up and not going straight for the nebuliser, but it's not time yet. I'm wearing my navy-blue hoody, Nik's spare black joggers (rolled up at the bottom) and my charcoal knitted beanie. Nik is similarly covered up in murky colours.

We follow the plan; all goes well until we pass a hawthorn hedge, and I have to suppress a fit of coughing (hawthorn pollen is my worst hay fever trigger). When we reach Willow Avenue, Nik checks that no one's watching us before gently opening Mr Gray's ornate iron gate.

We creep into the back garden. It's still, and completely quiet. The paving stones near the back door are packed with pots of plants.

Nik stops by the back door. He pauses for so long, I nudge his elbow. "What's up?" I whisper.

"I'm not sure we're doing the right thing. What if we get caught and I end up in prison? I bet DI Bell wouldn't understand us going to these lengths to find information – "

"Nik! This was your idea in the first place!" I'm annoyed that he's trying to put the brakes on just when we're getting to the good bit. "Of course we're doing the right thing. We're trying to find out the truth! That's always worth a risk, isn't it?"

"I don't know – "

"If we stand out here talking, we're going to attract attention, for sure. Let's see if there's a key. If there is, we go in. If not, we go home and quit." I cross my fingers in my pockets and watch as Nik slowly reaches up to the top of the door frame.

"Nope," he says. He sounds relieved.

"We've got to try under the pots," I say, not

letting him give up just yet.

Nik and I both get stuck in. He lifts one of the bigger terracotta pots, then another, and I tackle the smaller ones. After a few minutes – by which time I'm starting to feel a little bit panicky – Nik freezes.

"Here." He holds up a small, silver key, still wet from the watering Mr Gray must have given his plants before he left.

"OK. Well, there you go. Fate."

Nik's face is a mixture of dread and anticipation. "Fate. Yeah, I guess. Well, gloves on then. I'll wipe this key off, and in we go." He swallows noisily as he pulls the thin latex gloves slowly over his hands.

Mine are on in seconds. I take the key from his unresisting fingers and put it in the back door lock.

Chapter 13

The door opens silently as I turn the polished brass knob. We step inside and close the door behind us. The first thing I notice is the wooden floorboards gleaming in the sliver of moonlight that reaches them.

"Oh, my days," Nik says. "It's like a National Trust house!"

The house is beautiful, and as clean and neat as a museum. We walk towards the front of the house. In the hallway, the walls are wood panelled behind the bookcases, and the oak staircase twists to the first floor with a runner of red velvet carpet secured by brass stair rods on every step.

"It smells of something – a bit sweet – like candles and lavender bags," I say, sniffing as I follow Nik to the living room door.

"Polish, I expect," Nik says. "Where shall we look first?"

He checks behind every door leading from the hallway. "There's the office sort of library room here, then the kitchen and the living room, or we could go upstairs – ?"

"Let's start in the office," I say. I don't really fancy going too far from our escape route.

There are bookcases lining the walls, each one filled with leatherbound books with gold lettering; I see titles like *Leaves of Grass*, *Poetical Works of Lord Byron* and *The Ingoldsby Legends*. I've never heard of any of them. In the middle of the room is an antique desk, piled with papers and yet more books, and in the corners are tall cabinets with drawers, made of a dark, reddish wood.

I pick up one of the hardbacks on the desk. "*The Hobbit* by J. R. R. Tolkien," I read aloud.

"That's one of my favourites," Nik says, pausing his tour around the shelves. "Let's see." He opens the book and glances at the first page. Then he whistles, low and slow.

"What?" I ask, impatient to know what's so special.

"First edition. Worth a fortune. Much more than Dad's car, anyway." He puts the book back on the desk, very gently.

I don't dare touch any books after that, gloves or no gloves. The possibility of damaging something so expensive is way too scary.

We search in all the cupboards and filing cabinets in the office, among invoices and letters about book collections and receipts and all sorts of completely boring paperwork.

I try and make out the names of the books in Toni's pictures, to compare with the ones on the shelves, but the fuzzy old photos aren't clear enough to tell.

I move on to the living room. It's painted a deep greyish green, and the curtains are cream with a delicate leaf design. I admire the fireplace, with its coloured tiles and real wood ash collected under the grate. At each end of the mantelpiece there are tall silver candlesticks, with a fancy brass clock between them ticking regularly and really quite loudly.

The paintings on the wall are definitely the same as in Mrs Portendorfer's day. But – as Dad said – Mrs Portendorfer might have sold them to Mr Gray with the house.

All I can think is that we've wasted our time. There's nothing useful here. I *so* don't want to give up and go home empty-handed. My heart is beating hard, and my breathing is already laboured, when Nik comes in looking excited.

"This might be something," he says, holding out a piece of paper he's found in one of the drawers. "It's an agreement letter from Sunnyview Care Home in Welburton, referring to a Mrs Margery Gray. What are the chances that his mum or auntie had the same name as Mrs Portendorfer?"

I feel my eyes narrow. "Not that likely. Hang on to it, in case we find more information."

Nik goes back to the office to carry on sifting through the drawers.

I look around, and in that moment, I spot something that makes my spine tingle. A closed cupboard against the wall, behind an upright armchair.

There's a key in the cupboard door. It's tiny, made of polished brass, and it turns smoothly; I swing the door open.

Three Victorian porcelain dolls are sitting on a shelf staring blankly at me.

"Nik," I wheeze. "Those dolls! They're the ones in Mrs Finch's photo!"

Chapter 14

I reach out and touch the nearest doll. As I do, there's a strange and ghostly sound from the hallway.

… *ting* …

"What was that?" Nik says, freezing just inside the living room door.

"I don't know," I say, feeling frozen myself.

Nik turns around slowly. "Umm, there's a phone here, on the side table. I think this might be what made that sound."

We both go back into the hall and look at the phone. It's a very old-fashioned one, much older looking than the red one in the cupboard at home. It's black, made from a hard but not-quite-plasticky material, and has a weird shape; like a tall column rather than a squat cube, and supporting a strange trumpet-shaped receiver.

Nik lifts the receiver up and listens. "It's connected. I guess Mr Gray likes his modern conveniences as retro as possible."

I reply automatically: "It's Mrs Portendorfer's house, not Mr Gray's. Those dolls – they prove that something has happened to Mrs Portendorfer because she wouldn't have left them behind – and that Mr Gray is lying about not knowing who she is."

We're close. I can feel it. I exhale a long, trembling breath. "I was just touching one of the dolls, when the phone tinged," I said. "Stay here and I'll try it again."

I go back, put out my hand tentatively and tap a different doll. No reaction.

"Maybe it was just a coincidence," I say, starting to relax.

But then I put my hand on that first doll again.

... *ting* ...

I stifle my instinct to scream. "That wasn't a coincidence."

"It's got to mean something." Nik comes back into the living room, as I take the doll out of the cupboard.

She's got a sweet, fragile face and curled blonde hair, pink cheeks, a velvet dress and petite satin shoes. "No wonder Mrs Finch remembers playing with them," I say.

"Does the dress unbutton?" Nik asks. He's looking at the doll with a dubious expression. "If there's something here – it's going to be hidden. Or Mr Gray would've found it long ago."

I turn over the doll and examine her. Her clothes are stitched neatly and minutely with white thread, and she's wearing a lace bonnet over her curls. I carefully take this off, but nothing is underneath except hair.

Or – is there? I lift up the hair and look closely at the base of the doll's head. It's attached to the soft body, not with tiny, neat stitches but with large and untidy loops of grey cotton.

One end of this grey cotton is hanging loose, and I give it a tug. The seam falls apart as the thread comes easily out in one sliding motion. The smiling, porcelain head falls into Nik's waiting hand.

"There's something in there," I say, in a strained whisper.

I put in a finger and hook out a yellowing piece of folded paper. Nik leans in to get a good view as I unfold the paper with slightly trembling fingers.

Chapter 15

The paper is an official form, with the heading "Title Deeds". I struggle to make out the faded ink in the dim moonlight. It seems to say – in unnecessarily complicated legal language – that the land at 3 Willow Avenue belongs absolutely to Mr Michael and Mrs Margery Portendorfer of the same address.

Nik's voice has an odd crack in it when he speaks. "Well, this is proof of something, I'm sure of it, or why would it be hidden away?"

I'm just about to ask Nik what we should do next, when we're interrupted by a sharp, loud tapping on the front door. My hand flies to my mouth, while Nik looks around wildly.

We stand, frozen to the spot, for a long moment. Then we hear squeaking as the letter box is pushed open.

"Annie! Nik! Where are you?"

It's Dad! I can suddenly move again, but I'm not sure whether to be glad or sad that he's here. Nik seems to be looking for somewhere to hide, as I go slowly to the front door and turn the latch.

Dad's face is red, and he ducks quickly through the door and immediately starts telling Nik off in a loud whisper. "Nicholas William Edwards, how dare you bring your sister out to break into a stranger's house in the dead of night! Never in all my life would I have imagined you could be so reckless, so idiotic, so – "

"It's not Nik's fault, Dad! I wanted to come – "

"And as for you, Annie Edwards, I hope you don't think you're ever leaving the house without me again!"

"Dad, listen." Nik stands up straight, trying to be taken seriously.

But Dad's not in the mood to hear us. "Home, now. I don't want to hear another word from the pair of you. If I hadn't read your notebook, Annie, I'd have had to call the police! You can attempt to explain yourselves in the morning." Dad is so fierce that we give up trying to talk.

Nik and I exchange looks; I can see he's hiding something – probably the care home letter – in his pocket. I look behind me; the doll lies in pieces on Mr Gray's high-backed armchair. There's no chance to grab her, and Dad would probably explode if I tried to remove any of "Mr Gray's property" anyway.

I slip the house deeds into my own pocket, while Dad is opening the front door. There's a grey light in the sky; it's past 4 o'clock and the sun is starting to brighten the horizon a little.

We walk home in silence.

Breakfast next morning does not start well.

Dad is drinking coffee at the table when I come downstairs to grab my tablets. I'd normally ask him if he's ready for physio, but something about the look in his eyes makes me stay quiet.

Nik comes down ten minutes later, by which time I've made myself a bowl of porridge. His hair is a mess, and his eyes are a little pink. Mine might look similar; I don't remember sleeping much.

I hear Dad's intake of breath, now we're both here, ready to launch into his questions and rebukes.

"Are you ready to listen yet?" Nik asks. Something about his tone stops Dad's rant in its tracks.

"We found some things," I say, trying to copy Nik's calmness and serious air.

I tell Dad about the dolls and show him Mrs Finch's faded photo of them. I tell him Mrs Portendorfer would never have left them behind. Then I unfold the official house deeds. "Loads of the furniture is the same, and the paintings. I think something happened to Mrs Portendorfer, and

Mr Gray was involved."

Dad stares at the deeds. "I'm not sure it's absolute proof, Annie. But ... I think it's enough for me to call the police at Swinwood. We'll have to hope they won't press charges against you for breaking in, in light of this information."

Nik and I nod.

"You should probably ask for DI Bell," Nik says.

Dad raises an eyebrow but doesn't enquire further. Then he uses his mobile to call the hub. Within minutes, DI Bell has picked up his call and is asking Dad question after question.

I'm in a sort of daze, I guess, sitting in the kitchen while Dad tries to explain what we've done and what we've found.

"Right – see you shortly," he says, ringing off. He turns to me and sees I'm not quite myself. "Come here, Annie," he says, putting a comforting arm around me. "I don't approve of the way you two went about it, but it's possible you've made a difference in the world. DI Bell is on her way with a colleague to talk to you."

Nik goes upstairs to get dressed, but Dad and I stay in our hug for a while. The minutes tick by until there's a sudden rap on the front door. Nik rumbles down the stairs.

"Mr Edwards?" We can hear DI Bell call, and we both get up together.

"Good morning," she says, as she walks into the house. "This is DS Lee. Could you show us this certificate you've found, and tell us about where you found it?"

We're in as much trouble as we're ever likely to be, so I cross my fingers and pass it over.

"It was hidden in the head of a doll that we know belonged to Mrs Portendorfer and had great sentimental value for her," I say. "There was a *lot* of her stuff still in the house."

I also hand over the photographs we have from Mrs Finch, Toni and the estate agent. Nik hands over the back door key we found.

DI Bell sighs as she scans the deeds. "Well, this

raises questions. We'll have to get in touch with the Land Registry to find out if there's been an official change of ownership to this Mr Gray. We'll also need to see if there's any evidence of Mrs Portendorfer's movements after Mr Gray took residency of the house. I'll put some searches in motion."

A thought flashes through my mind – that care home! – and I catch Nik's eye. I think we both know that we ought to pass the letter to DI Bell, but neither of us speaks.

DS Lee murmurs something in DI Bell's ear. She looks up and nods at him. "Much as we appreciate this information," she then says to Dad, "we really can't overlook the way these two went about finding it. Trespassing on private property is a serious offence, even if you did find a key and there's no actual damage done. I will have to see whether there are any charges to be brought."

"But no one would ever have known there was something wrong!" I say, outraged. "Mrs Portendorfer would never have got justice if it was down to the police!"

Chapter 16

To my surprise, DI Bell smiles at me. "I can only imagine how you're all feeling. It's been a long night, but we've got this from here; we'll possibly need to get a warrant, and a forensics team to search the property."

DS Lee heads to the front door. "It's important to discover the truth," he says. "We'll be in touch when we find out more."

There's more silence after the police officers have gone. But not the frosty, enraged kind we shared last night.

Dad sighs, eventually, and rubs the back of his head. "We'd better do your physio, Annie.

And have you remembered your breathing exercises, in all this excitement?"

While we do those things, Nik eats his breakfast, and I find him waiting in my room when I drag my weary legs up the stairs afterwards.

"You didn't mention the care home letter," he says.

"Nor did you," I reply.

"Does that mean – "

"We should track it down ourselves? Yes." I knew Nik wouldn't let me down.

"What about Dad?" Nik says, biting his lip.

I take in a deep breath to soothe my jumping nerves. "He wouldn't be very happy with us if he knew we'd hidden evidence from DI Bell."

"No. Tell you what – let's see if we can find it online. And then decide what to do next."

Nik opens his personal laptop, which I have NEVER been allowed near, and while it's starting up, he gets out the letter we stole from 3 Willow Avenue.

"Sunnyview Care Home, Welburton." He types it into the search engine, as I hover behind his shoulder.

There are a fair number of results. None about a care home called Sunnyview, as such, although there are two: Ash Green Residential Care and The Beeches.

"I suppose it might have changed its name," I say. "If someone else bought it. It has been 48 years."

"Hold on," Nik says. He points to a map halfway down the screen showing an apartment building called Sunnyview House. "What if it got sold and converted into flats?"

"It might have. Shall we check it out? Welburton's only a few miles away along the ring road and there are buses. We've got three chances to find Sunnyview and see if there are any records." I give Nik my best pleading look, and he grins.

"I'll tell Dad we're going to play table tennis in the park. He'll be too busy watching the TV to worry, I reckon."

Nik's right. Dad is watching TV, but he won't let us go before we promise we're not going back to number 3. We aren't, so that's easy.

We walk quickly to the bus stop on Main Street. The Welburton bus arrives on time, even though it's a Sunday timetable, so we're soon on our way.

Welburton's a small town, so it's not impossible for us to walk to each of the addresses on our list once the bus has dropped us by the shopping centre. First, we head for Ash Green, which is the nearest.

The building is large and sprawling, and it takes us a few minutes to find the receptionist. She's reading a book, and the whole place seems quiet and snoozy.

"Hi," I say, when she looks up and smiles. "We have a slightly ... strange question. Did this place ever have a different name? We're looking for Sunnyview Care Home but the info we have is from nearly 50 years ago."

Gennie (or so says her name badge) creases her forehead in thought. "Not that I'm aware of.

Hold on, let me just ask Vick in the office. She's been here forever." She picks up her telephone and calls an internal number.

"Hi, Vick? Was Ash Green ever called Sunnyview? There are some young people here asking … Oh, right, OK. Thanks." Down went the phone with a ting that made me flinch.

"Not here, I'm afraid. This building went up in 1987, and before that there was a derelict mill on this site. Sorry."

I sigh heavily as we leave the home. "One down, two to go."

"Yes. Two more chances," Nik says. "Look on the bright side."

The apartment building isn't far – just a few turnings along the twisty terraced roads. When we get there, we're faced with a tall Victorian-style mansion house, set back off the road. There is a column of doorbells, each one labelled with the name of a resident, outside the gate.

"Who do we ask?" I say, looking at the list

of names and trying to decide which sounded most approachable.

"There might be a caretaker – " Nik says.

"One who's been here 50 years? I somehow doubt it."

Nik gets out his smartphone and opens a map app. "The Beeches is a seven-minute walk away. Let's try that first and then come back if all else fails. I don't want to annoy anyone, ringing all the bells."

Seven minutes later, we find ourselves outside our third gigantic building of the day. This one has clear signs to reception, and we're greeted by a cheerful, older man wearing gold-rimmed glasses.

"Well, hello there! You're new around here. How can I help you?"

I give Raymond a big smile (name badges are so useful). "We're looking for Sunnyview Care Home. I don't suppose this used to be it, did it?"

Raymond looks surprised when we mention Sunnyview. "That's not a name I've heard in a long

time," he says. "I've worked here for 27 years in all, and I remember Mrs Ackerman who ran this place for years and years before that, and she said she'd changed the name to sound more exclusive and grand. I think it's so she could charge more. Does that help you?"

Chapter 17

We've actually found it.

Nik gets out the letter and passes it over the desk to Raymond. "We're looking for any record of a woman called Margery Gray. We're interested to know when she arrived and any details there might be about her."

Raymond looks at the paper. "But this is very old – how long ago was she here?"

"Possibly the 1970s?" I say, thinking back to the telephone directory.

"Hmmm. Well, I know that our database only goes back 20 years or so – " He looks up at the ceiling. "But I do happen to know that Mrs Ackerman put a whole lot of paper files in one of the old storerooms. Everything's going to end up shredded, once the new management get round to it, but I wonder if there might be some records there – "

"Ooh, could you check?" I'm bouncing on my toes.

"Would it be a massive inconvenience?" Nik says, although I can see he's as keen as I am.

Raymond laughs. "Those records are so old, I don't think it could do any harm if I let you have a root around."

He shows us to a nearby room with a kettle and some soft chairs dotted about. "Staff tearoom," he says. "The storeroom's through here."

It smells dusty and a bit stale. Nik finds the light switch and I hear him give a little gasp as he takes in the piles of cardboard folders.

"Annie – perhaps you'd better put on your mask," he says. I pull it out of my pocket.

"Where do we start?" I ask. "Is there any sort of

order to these piles?"

"I hope so," Nik says. He shuffles around, scanning the cramped handwriting on the top of each folder. "Phew. There's a bit of an alphabetical pattern to it. Each folder looks like a patient file, and this here is K, the next one J, the one after looks like H."

"So – G is next!" I say, scanning the piles. "Green – Garrett – Graham – Gould – Goodman – "

"Give me a handful too, we'll get through them twice as quickly," Nik replies.

We're near the bottom of the pile before we find a surname we know. "Gray," Nik says. "Do you think – ?" He drops the rest of the folders he's holding. I abandon my own search, and we huddle together under the bare light bulb. The single sheet of paper in the folder tells us everything.

Mrs Margery Gray

Aged approx. 71 (DOB unrecorded).

Date of registration at Sunnyview: 23rd May 1976.

Placed here by her nephew, Mr Felix Gray, who has contracted to pay her service and accommodation fees for life.

Patient notes: Mr F. Gray reports that because of age-related dementia, his aunt has difficulty remembering who she is and where she lives. She may give alternative names or attempt to leave the premises if left unsupervised. She will need to be constantly reminded and taken great care of. Please ensure doors and windows are locked at night.

Contact address for F. Gray: 3 Willow Avenue, Macklemere.

Underneath is a stamp, in red ink: "Patient Deceased", with the handwritten date underneath it: 12th June 1979.

"Mrs Portendorfer died," I say, hardly able to speak with the grief gripping my throat. "Mr Gray *lied* and pretended Mrs Portendorfer was his aunt, and he left her here so he could take over her house. That's AWFUL."

Nik looks a bit wobbly too. "But we know the truth now, and we can take this back to DI Bell and then she's got the whole story. Proof at last of what a despicable human being Mr Gray is."

I try to pull myself together. I roll back my shoulders and wipe the wetness that has collected around my mask. "OK. Let's go home."

Chapter 18

Dad's not very impressed when we arrive home with the cardboard folder. Nik gets the worst of it, especially when I start crying again (I couldn't help it!), even though – as Nik keeps saying – getting a bus and going for a walk around a nearby town to visit care homes isn't even the second most dangerous thing we've ever done.

"I'm 18 years old, Dad. Annie was being accompanied by an adult the whole time."

Dad huffs and puffs for a while, but the new evidence soon distracts him. "I suppose the authorities weren't so hot on checking out people's identities back in those days. Mr Gray's even more of a villain than I imagined."

"Do you think they're already searching Mrs Portendorfer's house?" I ask. "We could take the folder round and see."

Dad nods. "Yes, let's do that. You coming, Nik?"

Nik looks outraged. "As if I'd miss it!"

DS Lee meets us at the front door of number 3 Willow Avenue. "I'm afraid we can't let anyone in until we've completed our sweep of the property – " he starts.

"It's OK! We just want to speak to DI Bell for a minute. Is she here?" Dad's tone is polite and apologetic, and the corner of DS Lee's mouth lifts slightly.

"Inspector!" he calls back into the hallway, and then DI Bell is there, with a questioning look on her face. "How can I help you? We did say we'd let you know if we found anything – "

"We know," Nik said. "But – "

"It's more that WE found something." I step forward and hold out the file.

"What's this?"

Dad tells her all about our trip to Welburton, and how we followed up the care home lead. He sounds really proud, which isn't what I was expecting after his earlier comments.

"I see," she says in the end. "So – you withheld something you found during your moonlight escapade in this house?"

I swallow anxiously, but then I realise she's smiling.

"I think this document adds to the chain of evidence. There's certainly enough to bring Mr Gray in for questioning. Well done, Annie – and Nik."

"What happens now?" I say.

"We'll carry on here. You go home, take a break from investigating; we'll be in touch to set up an appointment for you all to come in and make official statements."

She walks us the short distance to the pavement in front of Mr Gray's gate.

"Have you tracked down Mr Gray?" Nik says. "There can't be too many antiquarian book conferences taking place this weekend."

As he speaks, I catch a glimpse of movement, down at the bottom of the road. There's a tall, thin man holding a suitcase turning the corner at the far end of Willow Avenue. I gasp. I don't think it's loud, but the man looks up and stops, dead, when he sees the police cars and all the activity outside number 3. Before I can even squeak a warning to DI Bell, he's dropped the suitcase, turned on his heel and run back the way he came.

"That's him! He was just there!" I point in the right direction and DI Bell reacts immediately. She's young and fit, and she's racing down Willow Avenue to the corner in the blink of an eye. Chasing down the man who stole Mrs Portendorfer's life away from her.

Dad, Nik and I run after her as fast as we can, and as we reach that same corner a few seconds later, we're treated to an awesome sight. DI Bell has caught up with Mr Gray already – he's not wearing the right clothes or shoes for speed, after all – and she rugby-tackles him down into a pile of rubbish bags someone has left outside their house.

Dad and I give her a round of applause, as she reaches behind her belt for handcuffs and starts reading Mr Gray his rights. There's a smear of someone's leftover takeaway curry on his fancy jacket.

DI Bell marches Mr Gray back up Willow Avenue and deposits him in a police car.

"Well, that's that," she says to us, with a satisfied smile. "We'll take him to the station for questioning. Annie, thank you for all your help, and Nik too. You're both rather fine detectives."

Dad, Nik and I go back the next day to check in on Mrs Finch. Dad's even taken time off work! She knows most of the story from the police but is very impressed with how much Nik and I worked out on our own.

"DI Bell called us this morning to say that Mr Gray had finally confessed to putting Mrs Portendorfer in a home against her will and taking over the house. So, he'll definitely be going to prison, and Mrs Portendorfer's house will be returned to her remaining family," I say. "We might get to meet her great-niece, Toni, if she comes over from Australia."

"Good! And I'll tell you something," Mrs Finch says, "I'll find out where she's buried. There's bound to be a note of it in the local archives. I'll find Mrs P's grave and make sure it's marked with her real name."

On our way home, Dad says. "So, Annie, what are you going to do now?"

I shrug. "I'm not sure. I finished writing up the case in my notebook yesterday and filled in the others on the group chat. I wonder, though – "

"What?"

"If there are any more phone numbers in that notepad in the cupboard?"

Book talk questions

Which of the characters did you relate to the most?

Who was your favourite character in the book?

Would you have done anything differently than Annie and Nik?

Have you ever solved a mystery?

What other calls do you think the Time Travel Telephone might contain?

Do you like reading stories about a crime? Why?

What do you think about Mr Gray? Why do you think he behaved the way he did?

Why do you think Dad is so sceptical of the telephone?

Ask the author

How did you first get into writing?

I always thought of myself as a reader, not a writer, so I didn't even try until I spotted a newspaper advert for a children's novel competition in 2010. I thought I'd give writing a go, and I got the writing bug (I did NOT win the competition, sadly).

Lis Jardine

How did you come up with the concept of a telephone connected to the past?

I watched a TV series called *James May: The Reassembler,* where the TV presenter puts a piece of vintage technology together from all its tiny components. At the end of the "Telephone" episode, he said something about how he'd always had the strange feeling that if you picked up the handset of one of those old telephones you might hear the last call it made … and voilà. Instant inspiration (thanks James).

What is your favourite illustration in the book?
They are all brilliant, and I'm so completely in love with Alexandra's artwork! If I must pick one, it might be Mr Gray answering the door – he's so exactly right (that grim and grumpy expression!).

Did anyone inspire you for the character of Annie?
I'm a secondary school librarian, so I meet a lot of bright, inquisitive 11-year-olds and find them endlessly inspiring. I did particularly keep my three cousins in mind as I was writing Annie, though – Peter, Iain and Ed all have cystic fibrosis and lead creative and active lives despite the challenges of the condition. I'm in awe of their fortitude, and I wanted to portray some of the realities of a childhood with CF as best I could, in their honour.

What do you hope that readers get out of this book?
Peril, suspense, the puzzle of putting the clues together … More than anything, I hope readers get joy and pleasure out of their reading experience and want to pick up another book straight away.

Published by Collins
An imprint of HarperCollins*Publishers*

The News Building
1 London Bridge Street
London SE1 9GF
UK

Macken House
39/40 Mayor Street Upper
Dublin 1
D01 C9W8
Ireland

Text © Lis Jardine 2025
Design and illustrations © HarperCollins*Publishers* Limited 2025

10 9 8 7 6 5 4 3 2 1

ISBN 978-0-00-874489-2

British Library Cataloguing-in-Publication Data
A catalogue record for this publication is available from the British Library.

Author: Lis Jardine
Illustrator: Alexandra Pulga (Astound)
Publisher: Laura White
Commissioning editor: Holly Woolnough
Development editor: Zoë Clarke
Product manager: Holly Woolnough
Content editor: Selin Akca
Copyeditor: Sally Byford
Proofreader: Catherine Dakin
Reviewer: Lisa Davis
Cover designer: Sarah Finan
Internal design: 2Hoots Publishing Services Ltd
Typesetter: Jouve India Ltd
Production controller: Katharine Willard

Collins would like to thank the teachers and children at Grange Primary School, Southwark, for being part of the development of Big Cat Read On.

With thanks to Cystic Fibrosis Trust for their help reviewing this book.

Printed in the UK.

MIX
Paper | Supporting
responsible forestry
FSC™ C007454

Get the latest Collins Big Cat news at
collins.co.uk/collinsbigcat